JAMIE SMART'S

MACHINE MAYHEM!

David Fickling Books

The comics in this book were originally published in The Phoenix Comic.

Adaptation, additional artwork and colours by Sammy Borras.
Cover design by Paul Duffield and Jamie Smart.

Bunny vs Monkey: Machine Mayhem
is a
DAVID FICKLING BOOK

First published in Great Britain by
David Fickling Books,
31 Beaumont Street,
Oxford, OX1 2NP

Hardback edition published 2022
This edition published 2023

Text and illustrations © Jamie Smart, 2022

978-1-78845-297-7

1 3 5 7 9 10 8 6 4 2

The right of Jamie Smart to be identified as the author and illustrator of this work
has been asserted in accordance with the Copyright, Designs and Patents Act 1988.

All rights reserved. No part of this publication may be reproduced, stored in a retrieval system,
or transmitted in any form or by any means, electronic, mechanical, photocopying,
recording or otherwise, without the prior permission of the publishers.

Papers used by David Fickling Books are from well-managed forests
and other responsible sources.

MIX
Paper from
responsible sources
FSC® C104723
FSC
www.fsc.org

DAVID FICKLING BOOKS Reg. No. 8340307

A CIP catalogue record for this book is available from the British Library.

Printed and bound in China by Toppan Leefung.

D.I.WHYYYY?

AFTER ALL THE CALAMITY OF LAST YEAR, IT WAS NICE TO JUST SIT DOWN, RELAX, AND ENJOY OUR WOODS...

I'M READY TO DO SOME NAILIN', BUNNY!

GREAT STUFF!

MY FRIENDS ALL PITCHED IN AND WORKED HARD TO REBUILD MY HOUSE...

9

10

11

14

15

22

"THE HOUSEMATE"

HEY, I'M JOINING YOU IDIOTS NOW.

UHH, I THOUGHT YOU HUNG OUT WITH SKUNKY ALL THE TIME?

NOPE. HE'S BUSY WORKING ON SOME SECRET PROJECT AND HE KICKED ME OUT.

YOU THERE! PACK MY THINGS AWAY, WON'T YOU?

HANG ON, NO. NO NO NO!

YOU HAVE YOUR OWN HOME — THERE! THE POD YOU CRASHED IN!

BUT IT SMELLS LIKE FARTS.

WELL, WHOSE FAULT IS THAT?

...

G...

GOBLINS?

"ROBOT RAMPAGE"

BEHOLD! THE FUTURE OF EVIL ROBOTICS!

METAL E.V.E.

WHAT DOES E.V.E. STAND FOR?

EXTRA...

VROBOT...

...EEK?

EEKING.

EEKING?

LOOK, I SPENT A LONG TIME BUILDING HER. I DIDN'T HAVE TIME TO FIGURE HER NAME OUT TOO.

31

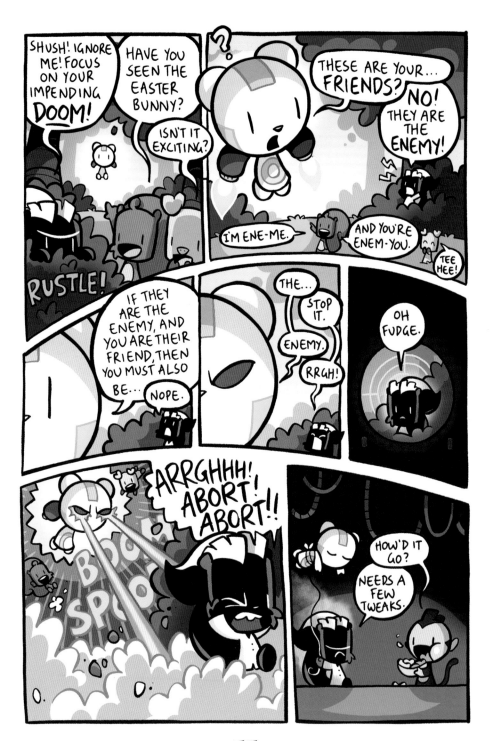

33

AFTER YOUR HORRIFIC CRASH IN MY **FIREBALL 5000**...

T-T-THIS W-W-WAS A-A-A B-B-BAD I-I-IDEA!

YOU WERE SO BADLY INJURED, I HAD TO FIND A WAY TO REVIVE YOU!

SO I INVENTED THE **LAZARUS PYRAMID!**

YOUR BANDAGES ARE LACED WITH **REVIVE-B**, A LIQUID DERIVED FROM CATERPILLAR COCOONS. IT HELPS YOUR CELLS TO REGROW AT AN **ACCELERATED RATE!**

STOP RUINING EVERYTHING WITH SCIENCE! I'M A **MUMMY.**

A MUMMY.

A MONKEY.

IT'S PRONOUNCED **MONKEY.**

DUSTY POO TO YOU, I AM A **MUMMY!** DOOMED TO WALK THE EARTH AND...

FLUMP!

37

40

41

43

44

45

A DANGEROUS VOYAGE

49

50

WAIT, **WHY** AM I DOING THIS?

SIGHHH, I ALREADY **TOLD** YOU!

WHILE ACTION BEAVER WAS ON GUARD, THE **LASERTRONOTRON** WENT MISSING FROM MY LABORATORY. HE, HOWEVER, CANNOT RECALL WHO TOOK IT. SO, I MUST SHRINK YOU, AND FIRE YOU INSIDE HIS BRAIN TO FIND THE MEMORY!

BAZOINK.

SEE? HE EXPLAINS IT BETTER THAN I COULD!

58

59

... A MILLION CALCULATIONS A SECOND...

YOU **ATE** THEM! YOU *GREEDY FLOPSY!* YOU ATE ALL OF SKUNKY'S HARD WORK!

BLURGH!

AND NOW I HAVE TO RECAPTURE THEM ALL BEFORE HE GETS BACK!

SOME HOURS LATER...

WE'RE BACK FROM FISHING!

I CAUGHT A **TOILET.**

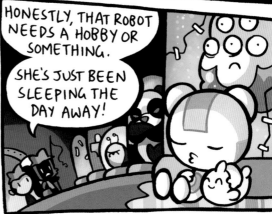

HONESTLY, THAT ROBOT NEEDS A HOBBY OR SOMETHING.

SHE'S JUST BEEN SLEEPING THE DAY AWAY!

65

66

67

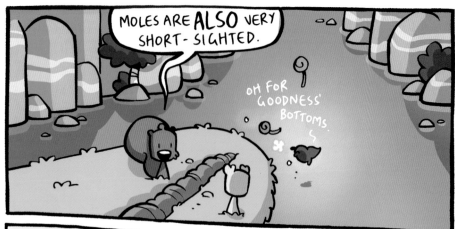

MOLES ARE **ALSO** VERY SHORT-SIGHTED.

OH FOR GOODNESS' BOTTOMS.

A LOUD SPLOOSH LATER...

THERE YOU GO, ROLAND.

SAFELY BACK ON LAND.

SPLUHH SPLUH!!

AWW, BUT THE FLOWERS ARE ALL WET NOW!

I'VE SPOILT IT FOR ALL OF US!

NEVER MIND, WE CAN **SHARE** THE SOGGY FLOWERS. THAT'S A GOOD LESSON FOR US ALL TO LEARN TODAY.

THE IMPORTANCE OF **SHARING.**

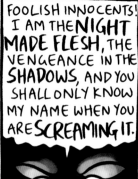

FOOLISH INNOCENTS! I AM THE **NIGHT MADE FLESH,** THE VENGEANCE IN THE **SHADOWS,** AND YOU SHALL ONLY KNOW MY NAME WHEN YOU ARE **SCREAMING IT.**

WHAT?

SHARING.

AHHH. SHARING.

68

69

I COME FROM A DIMENSION WHERE WE **DIDN'T** USE THE DEVICE, AND AS A RESULT OUR ENTIRE REALITY IS NOW MADE OF **CHEESE!**

OOOH.

WHY... WHY'S IT MADE OUT OF CHEESE?

IT'S COMPLICATED, AND I'M NOT ENTIRELY SURE. THE POINT IS YOU **HAVE** TO USE THAT DEVICE!

IF YOU DON'T, THEN WE'LL ALL...

WAIT!

YOU **DID** USE THE DEVICE. JUST NOW, TO OPEN THAT PORTAL AND COME HERE!

I DID? OH NO! I DID!

SO...WAIT. WHAT DOES THAT MEAN?

DO I USE THE DEVICE OR NOT?

GIVE ME A MINUTE.

EVERYONE! STOP DITHERING!

BLO ORP!

I AM FROM A DIMENSION WHERE OUR **INDECISIVENESS** CAUSED A MASSIVE DISRUPTION IN THE FABRIC OF SPACE-TIME!

THE ONLY OUTCOME WE'VE NOTICED, HOWEVER...

72

"BEAVERVILLE"

WELCOME, TRAVELLER, TO THE CITADEL OF BEAVER-VILLE!!

I AM THE GATEKEEPER, SOVEREIGN HOLDER OF THE BEAVER STAFF, FOURTH APPOINTED EARL OF BEAVERVILLE.

AND YOU ARE....?

FFF-TING!

FFF-TING?

YOUR NAME IS FTUNGG?

FTUNGG!

PRRP BLIP BLIP HONK!

WELL, MISTER BLIP BLIP HONK, IT WAS VERY FORTUITOUS THAT I FOUND YOU OUT THERE IN THE WOODS, ROLLING IN FOX MUCK...

...FOR NOW I CAN SHOW YOU ALL THE SPLENDOURS OF **BEAVERKIND!**

THESE ARE OUR **SOLDIER BEAVERS**. THEY TRAVEL INTO THE DARKEST LANDS AND FIND MORE WOOD FOR OUR CAUSE.

AND THESE ARE **WORKER BEAVERS**, WHO CHEW THAT WOOD INTO THE **PERFECT THICKNESS!**

DRKRRRK RRRR!

PERFECT FOR **WHAT**, I HEAR YOU ASK?

WELL, I'LL SHOW YOU.

PRRP?

74

HERE IN BEAVERVILLE, WE DEVOTE OUR LIVES TO BUILDING A **WOODEN TOWER**, RISING TOWARDS, AND INTO, THE HEAVENS!

AND WHEN WE MAKE IT TO THE VERY, VERY TOP WE ARE GOING TO HAVE SUCH A PARTY!

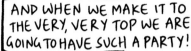

HANG ON—**WHY** ARE WE BUILDING THIS TOWER?

HERETIC!

NO ONE QUESTIONS THE TOWER. IF WE DID, WE'D REALISE THAT WE DON'T ACTUALLY KNOW THE ANSWER.

AND THAT WOULD JUST BE STUPID.

FORTUNATELY FOR **YOU**, HOWEVER, MISTER BLIP BLIP HONK, WE DO NOW HAVE A VACANCY FOR A NEW WORKER BEAVER!

SO? WHAT DO YOU SAY?

"ROFL AXOLOTL"

MONKEY, IF THIS IS ABOUT UNBLOCKING YOUR TOILET AGAIN, I ALREADY TOLD YOU, **NO**. YOU MAY **NOT** BORROW MY TOOTHBRUSH.

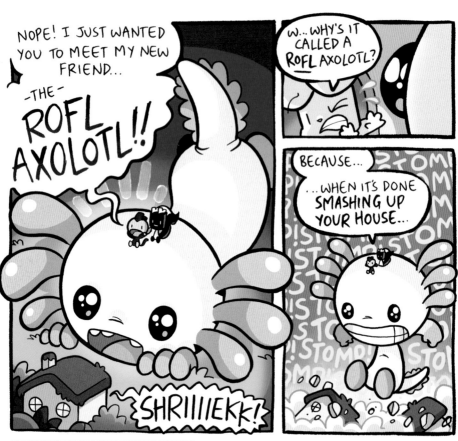

79

80

84

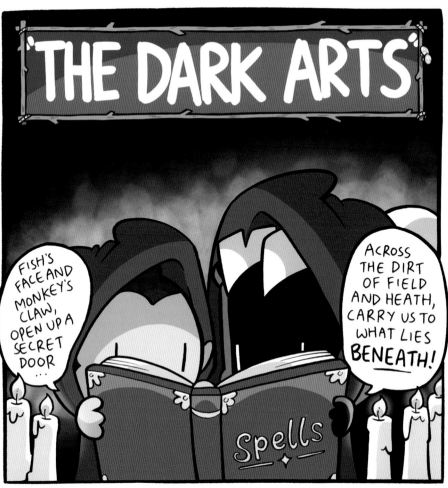

87

"GLOOBS"

MISTER SKUNKY DESIGNED US! HE REALISED THAT PERHAPS MONKEY DOESN'T ACTUALLY NEED TO **BECOME** A KING, HE JUST NEEDS TO BE **TOLD** HE IS ONE.

YAH YAH! BORING WORDS. ONE OF YOU BAKE ME A CAKE!

YES, SIRE!

SIRE! IT'S THE BEST I COULD DO IN THE TIME!

MEH. IT'LL DO. I'LL SLAM MY FACE INTO IT LATER.

UR FACE!

CLAP CLAP CLAP CLAP CLAP!!

THEY'RE APPLAUDING ME FOR DOING A **POO!**

CLAP CLAP CLAP CLAP!!

I THINK THIS IS THE MOST PERFECTLY DELIGHTFUL SPOT FOR A PICNIC!

I DO TOO!

MUNCH MUNCH

OUT OF THE WAY! KING MONKEY WANTS TO STAND HERE!

HOI!

OW!

91

92

94

95

96

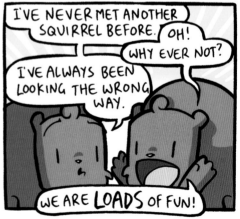

99

WEENIE MET ANOTHER SQUIRREL AND FORGOT ALL ABOUT ME.

OHHH, IS THAT ALL?

YOU SHOULD DO WHAT I DO AT TIMES LIKE THESE...

WHAT'S THAT?

BE AN ABSOLUTE BUM-FACE ABOUT EVERYTHING!

CRUMP!

WINNIE TOUCHED THE WEENIE-BALL!

SHE LOST THE GAME!

RUN AWAY!

RUN AWAY!

SHRIEK!

SHRIEK!

SHRIEK!

102

107

111

112

MAYBE YOU DON'T NEED A JELLYWISH TO BE A LITTLE BRAVER, A LITTLE QUIETER, OR FOR FRIENDS TO APPEAR.

117

118

120

OF COURSE IT WAS! I HID **TRACKING DEVICES** IN EACH OF THE BURGERS SO, ONCE CONSUMED, WE CAN SEE WHERE OUR ENEMIES ARE AT ANY GIVEN MOMENT!

AND LOOK! WE'RE PICKING UP THEIR READINGS ALREADY!

BOOP! BOOP!

WE WILL PURSUE THEM! **RELENTLESSLY! DOGGEDLY!**

THEY ALL SEEM TO BE GOING DOWN RIVER!

DON'T LET THEM GET AWAY!

PHEW! YOU WERE WISE TO NOT EAT THE BURGERS, PIG! THEY WENT **RIGHT THROUGH US!**

HEY, WHERE DID MONKEY AND SKUNKY GO?

YUM!

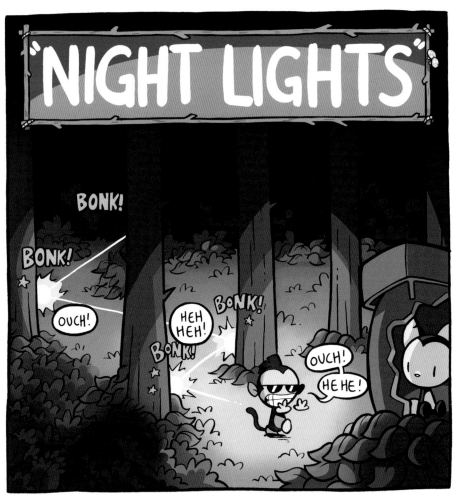

AND SO THEY BOTH WALKED, SUNGLASSES ON, THROUGH THE NIGHT...

"UPGRADES"

HOW IS AN EVIL GENIUS SUCH AS MYSELF SUPPOSED TO CREATE THE MOST MANIACAL AND HEIIIIINOUS CONTRAPTIONS THE WORLD HAS EVER SEEN IF HE IS STARVED OF THAT MOST ESSENTIAL OF FUELS...

...A GOOD CUP OF TEA!?

I LOVE UNICORNS

WHAT?

I'M NOT MAKING YOU ONE.

THEN WHAT DID I DESIGN YOU FOR?

I WISH I KNEW! YOU CREATED ME TO BE SUPER EFFICIENT, BUT GAVE ME NO PURPOSE!

NOW MY MEMORY NODULES HAVE CORRODED WITH THE BOREDOM.

PURPOSE? WELL, IF IT'S PURPOSE YOU WANT...

129

135

136

"FLUFFY"

THERE'S A DOG IN THE WOODS!

YIP! YIP! YIP! YIP! YIP! YIP! YIP! YIP! YIP! YIP! YIP! YIP!

A DOG!

HOW DID IT GET HERE?

YIP! YIP! YIP! YIP! YIP! YIP!

WHAT DOES IT DO?

IT DOES THIS!

YEEEEEEE!!

MY TURN! MY TURN!

KISS! KISS!

KISS

HA HA! IT'S VERY...

HANG ON.

YIP! YIP! YIP! YIP! YIP!

THERE'S A DOG IN MY HOUSE!!

CRASH! SMASH! YIP!

AND IT HAS MY **BLANKEY.**

RRR!

MY BLANKEY!

RRR!

MINE!

DRAGGGG!

HE'S PROBABLY JUST HUNGRY! BESIDES BLANKEY, WHAT DO DOGS LIKE TO EAT?

CAKE? JELLY? SPAGHETTI? DUCK A L'ORANGGGE?

SECONDS LATER... AT LEAST HE DIDN'T EAT MY HAT TOO.

HE ATE MY HAT TOO.

140

"DOWN BELOW"

WOULD YOU MIND TURNING OFF YOUR LIGHT, BUNNY?

I'M TRYING TO GET TO SLEEP.

LOOK, SKUNKY, HOW LONG EXACTLY ARE YOU PLANNING TO STAY AT MY HOUSE?

I TOLD YOU, UNTIL MY SECRET LAIR IS, UH... FUMIGATED.

BUGS. LOTS OF BUGS.

EW.

BUGS.

I DON'T BELIEVE YOU. YOUR LAIR'S NOT BEING FUMIGATED AT ALL.

WHY DO YOU REALLY NOT WANT TO GO BACK THERE?

FINE. FINE!

I'M HIDING FROM THE ALL-POWERFUL SUPER-COMPUTER I CREATED.

ALL-POWERFUL, MY BUM. C'MON, WE'RE GOING TO SORT THIS OUT TOGETHER.

BUT YOU HAVEN'T SEEN HER. YOU DON'T KNOW WHAT YOU'RE DEALING WITH!

YEAH? WELL NEITHER DOES SHE.

BECAUSE I AM STRONG. I AM DETERMINED. I AM A LITTLE BIT GRUMPY.

BUT MOST OF ALL, I AM BRAVE.

AT SKUNKY'S LAIR...

DID YOU... REDECORATE?

148

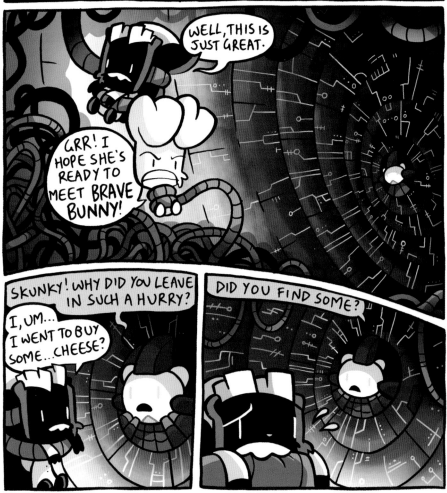

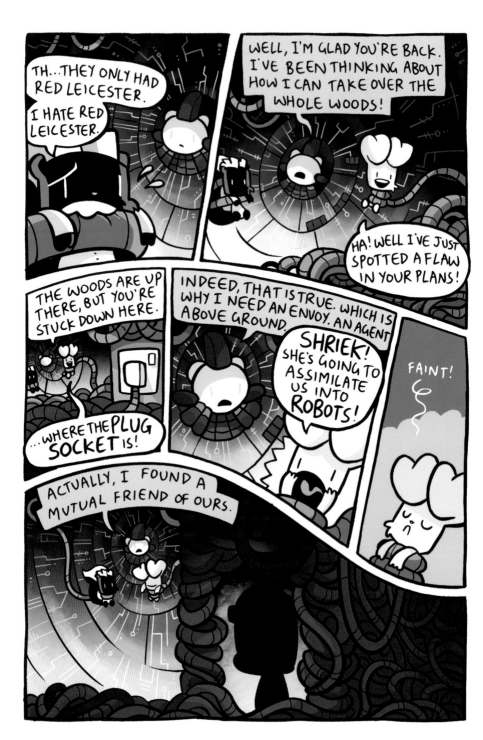

150

151

"PIG-KIRA!"

THERE HE IS!

EVE'S HENCHMAN...

...METAL STEVE!

...AND HE'S CARRYING THE **NANO-CANNON 3000!**

MY MOSTEST INGENIOUS INVENTION TO DATE...

...USED AGAINST ME!

NANO-WHAT?

NO, NANO-**BOTS!** THEY'RE MINUSCULE LITTLE ROBOTS ALL FLOATING INSIDE A CLOUD. THEY'LL TURN WHATEVER THEY TOUCH INTO **ROBOTS!**

IS HE GOING TO TURN <u>US</u> INTO ROBOTS?

'SOME KIND OF PLAN'

YOU CAN HEAR IT AT NIGHT...

THE GRINDING, THE BUZZING...

THE SOUNDS OF MACHINATIONS...

SOMETHING TERRIBLE OCCURRING BENEATH THE SOIL...

SOMETHING BEING BORN...

HERE IT IS! THE **BACK DOOR** TO MY SECRET LABORATORY!

WELL, LET'S CRACK IT OPEN!

WHAT ON EARTH DO YOU THINK IS GOING ON DOWN THERE?

BESIDES, EVER SINCE EVE TOOK OVER MY LABORATORY, ALL I HAVE LEFT IS WHATEVER'S IN MY POCKETS.

LET'S SEE...

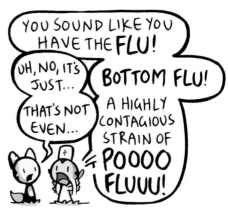

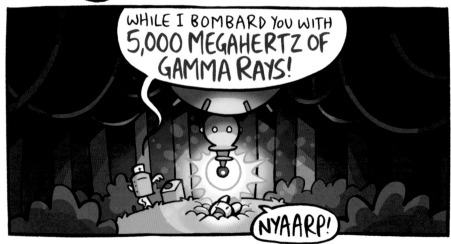

163

165

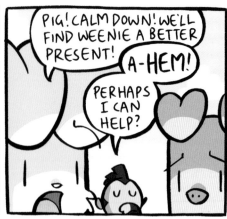

"SOMETHING TO SAY"

HAPPY BIRTHDAY, WEENIE!!

YAYY!

A SURPRISE PARTY? I HAD NO IDEA!

THANKS FOR BAKING THE CAKE, BY THE WAY.

IT'S FINE.

HERE, WEENIE, OPEN MY PRESENT FIRST!

HE'S GOING TO LOVE IT!

NO, OPEN MINE!

I BET HE LOVES MINE MORE!

FOR HE'S A JOLLY GOOD FELLOW, FOR HE'S A JOLLY GOOD FELLOW, FOR HE...

WEENIE? WHAT'S WRONG?

175

POSITIVE. I EVEN INVENTED A GIANT SAUCER OF MILK TO GO WITH HER.

SNUFFLE!
UFFLE!

SNUFFLE!
SNUFFLE!

THERE'S A GOOD GIRL.

PAT PAT!

HE'S... SUBDUING THE HEDGEHOG BOT?

ACTIVATE SPINES!

SCREEEEEEE EEE FEE!

PSCHEWWW!

PSCHWWWW!

PSCHEW!

PSCHEW!

181

186

187

189

191

SOMETIMES, AT NIGHT, WHEN I LOOK OUT OF MY WINDOW I CAN SEE A **GLOWING FIGURE** WALKING AROUND.

HAUNTING THE WOODS!

OH, THAT'S JUST ACTION BEAVER SLEEPWALKING.

HE'S **RADIOACTIVE** YOU KNOW.

ZZZP...

BONK..

ZZ...

GROOANN!

RIGHT, I GIVE UP. YOU'VE ALL SPOILT THIS GAME.

GROOO-ANNN!!

AND **WHO** KEEPS GROANING?

GROOOANN.

SCREEAMM!

I WON THE GAME!

196

198

200

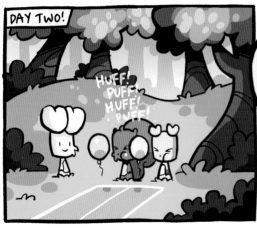

"AN OLD FRIEND"
WELCOME, WOODLAND ANIMALS, TO THE 534TH ANNUAL BALLOON RACE!
FINISH
COMPETITORS, READY!
BALLOONS, READY!
PHEEP!
AAAND... GO!!
HUFF!
PUFF!

202

SO, CONCEALED BY MY GHOSTLY FORM, I CARRIED PIG'S BALLOON OVER ZE FINISH LINE!

FINISH

THEN I BURST IT. OUT OF SPITE.

BUT, LE FOX! YOU DISAPPEARED INTO ANOTHER DIMENSION!

WELL... I CAME BACK.

I DON'T UNDERSTAND ZE RULES EITHER.

SOME OF THEM GET MADE UP AS WE GO ALONG.

ALL I KNOW IS THAT I INHABIT ZESE WOODS AS AN ETHEREAL FORM, A SPIRIT, POWERFULLY CONNECTED TO ZE...

SIGHHH.

FINE.

"CLASH OF THE ROBOTS"

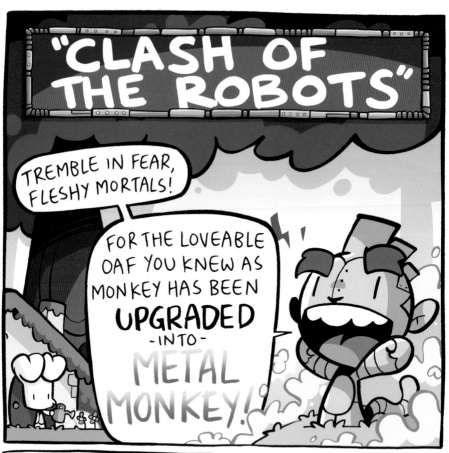

TREMBLE IN FEAR, FLESHY MORTALS!

FOR THE LOVEABLE OAF YOU KNEW AS MONKEY HAS BEEN **UPGRADED** -INTO- METAL MONKEY!

MONKEY, YOU... YOU BECAME A **ROBOT**?!

THAT I DID. PRETTTTTTY SNAZZY, HUH?

EVE WANTS TO TURN US ALL INTO ROBOTS ANYWAY. HOW DOES YOU BEATING HER TO IT HELP US AT **ALL**?

IT...

DOESN'T.

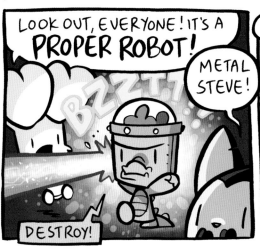

205

SUGGESTED SOUNDTRACK:
BEEP-BEEP BOOP BOOP

HAR HAR! RIGHT! NOW TO PUT EVERYTHING I'VE LEARNT INTO ACTION!

BRING ME... A TIN OF TUNA!!

BZZZZZZZZ!

YOU LEARNT... HOW TO BE A TIN OPENER?

YEAHHH! SO WATCH OUT.

207

208

209

210

211

214

YOU'D BE BRILLIANT AT IT.

BWOOP!

PAF!

BWOOP!

PAF!

SHRIEK! NO FAIR!

PAF!

BWOOP!

LE FOX CAN JUST POP UP ANYWHERE!

HMMM...

HE CAN, CAN'T HE.

BWOOP!

PAF!

DEEP, DEEP BELOW THE WOODS...

SO, MY TWO ROBOT ENVOYS. WHAT INFORMATION DO YOU BRING ME?

I FOUND OUT THAT I CAN FIT **ALL** MY TOES IN MY MOUTH.

WELL, I GUESS THAT'S USEFUL— AN INTRUDER!

BWOOP!

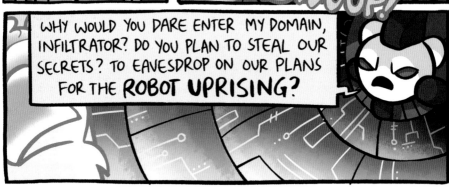

WHY WOULD YOU DARE ENTER MY DOMAIN, INFILTRATOR? DO YOU PLAN TO STEAL OUR SECRETS? TO EAVESDROP ON OUR PLANS FOR THE **ROBOT UPRISING?**

NAH.

PAF!

216

219

YEAHHH! I FINALLY LEARNT LASER EYES!

I'M A PROPER ROBOT!

NOW BOW DOWN TO YOUR ROBOT OVERLORRRRRRRRRR :-

SORRY, HE WASN'T FULLY CHARGED.

WE'LL BE BACK IN A BIT.

RISE OF THE MACHINES!

POSTPONED

YAY FOR MONKEY'S INADEQUATE BATTERY LIFE!

YAYY!

220

"PRESENTS"

MID-DECEMBER, AND IN ONE LITTLE POCKET OF THE WOODS A FESTIVE SCENE IS UNFOLDING...

IS IT CHRISTMAS ALREADY?!

NOT YET, PIG. BUT WE'VE BEEN GETTING READY FOR IT.

WITH A ROBOT APOCALYPSE ON THE WAY, WE MIGHT HAVE TO CELEBRATE IT EARLY!

I MADE MINI CHRISTMAS PUDDINGS! EACH HAS A LITTLE GIFT INSIDE!

IS...IS THIS A SHOE?

AND I'VE BEEN LAYING OUT THESE LIGHT-UP ELVES!

OH YAY!

BWOOM

THEY FIRE DEATH RAYS!

OH, THIS IS ALL SO EXCITING! CHRISTMAS IS THE MOST MAGICAL TIME OF THE YEAR!

I DON'T WANT TO RUIN YOUR FUN.

BUT THOSE ARE SOME DARK LOOKING CLOUDS.

223

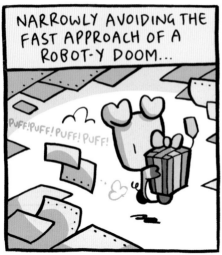

NARROWLY AVOIDING THE FAST APPROACH OF A ROBOT-Y DOOM...

PUFF! PUFF! PUFF! PUFF!

ALL TO DELIVER A PRESENT...

...TO ONE WHO HAD DONE NOTHING TO DESERVE IT.

SECRET ROBOT LAIR

TO THE ARCHITECT OF THEIR DEMISE.

WE HAVE TO GO AFTER HIM!

IT'S TOO DANGEROUS.

IT'S TOO DANGEROUS FOR ANY OF US.

226

YOU HAVE A NICE BEDROOM.

THIS IS NOT MY BEDROOM, PIG.

FROM INSIDE HERE I CAN OBSERVE EVERY INCH OF THE WOODS. EVERY MICROCOSMIC ACTION AND REACTION. NATURE AS ONES AND ZEROES.

I CAN EVEN REPLICATE IT ALL OUT OF PIXELS. IN MY EFFORTS TO UNDERSTAND LIFE, I SYNTHESISED GREAT FIELDS OF IT.

AND THEN I WATCHED IT ALL TURN TO DUST.

OVER AND OVER AGAIN.

FOR LIFE IS FRAGILE.

AND MUST BE PRESERVED.

I SHALL SAVE THIS WORLD.

BY ENCASING IT INSIDE METAL.

I GOT SOCKS FOR CHRISTMAS.

WERE YOU... WERE YOU LISTENING TO ANYTHING I SAID?

I'M A PIG. PIGS DON'T WEAR SOCKS.

230

231

I HAD TO SNEAK IT IN SOMEHOW. BUT FIRST, I HAD TO LAY THE BAIT FOR PIG SO HE WOULD COME DOWN HERE AND CHANGE YOUR MIND ABOUT TAKING OVER THE WORLD, THUS... MAKING IT SAFE FOR ME TO ENTER.

SO NOW I CAN PLUG THE STICK INTO YOUR USB-PORT NOSE...

CLICK!

AND REMOVE THE ONE FILE YOU DON'T NEED ANY MORE.

A THIRST TO TAKE OVER THE WORLD

USB

I DON'T UNDERSTAND. HOW DID YOU KNOW PIG WOULD CHANGE MY MIND?

OH, THAT'S EASY...

I KNEW THE BEST WAY TO DEFEAT THE MOST SOPHISTICATED CREATURE IN THE WORLD...

...WOULD BE WITH THE SIMPLEST ONE.

QUACK.

"TIDYING UP"

LOOK, I DON'T HAVE TIME FOR THIS. ARE YOU GOING TO TURN ME BACK INTO A NORMAL MONKEY OR NOT?

FINE. **FINE!**

SINCE EVE LET ME HAVE MY LABORATORY BACK, I HAVE FULL ACCESS TO ALL MY INVENTIONS AGAIN!

INCLUDING...THE RE-FLESHINATOR! IT'LL RETURN ANY ALTERED LIFEFORM INTO ITS ORIGINAL PHYSICAL FORM.

SHOOF!

I PUT A BANANA IN THERE FOR YOU.

OOH!

BANANA!

RIGHT! ARE YOU READY?

YES! FIRE IT UP QUICKLY BEFORE I NEED THE TOILET AGAIN!

THE END!

METAL STEVE

①

LIKE A LOT OF THE CHARACTERS IN BUNNY VS MONKEY, STEVE'S HEAD STARTS LIKE THIS...

...A **BULGING SQUARE!**

②

IN PENCIL, ADD A CROSS TO HELP YOU WORK OUT WHERE TO DRAW STEVE'S FACE!

③

WE CAN THEN ADD STEVE'S **EYES** ON THE HORIZONTAL PENCIL LINE.

④

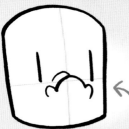

AND STEVE'S **SNOUT**, WHERE THE TWO LINES CROSS.

⑤

LETS ADD A COUPLE OF SHARP **TEETH** AND A **SMILE**.

⑥

NEXT, THE METAL BAND AT THE TOP OF STEVE'S HEAD, STUDDED WITH **SPIKES!**

⑦

THEN THE GLASS BOWL ABOVE IT. THIS WILL HOLD STEVE'S **BRAINS!**

⑧

(STEVE'S BRAINS ARE JUST A LUMPY PURPLE JELLY)

⑨

LASTLY, DRAW A LINE DOWN THE SIDE OF HIS FACE, AND ADD A FEW DOTS, TO MAKE HIM LOOK EVEN MORE ⚡**ROBOTIC!**⚡

HOW TO DRAW
METAL E.V.E.

① EVE'S HEAD IS DIFFERENT FROM STEVE'S... IT'S LIKE A SLIGHTLY **SQUASHED CIRCLE!**

② HER EARS ARE LITTLE ROUND LUMPS ON TOP OF HER HEAD.

③ ONE ON THE LEFT, ONE ON THE RIGHT, AND NOW LET'S DRAW HER **FACE...**

④

AGAIN, WE'LL PENCIL A LITTLE CROSS TO WORK OUT WHERE EVE IS LOOKING..

⑤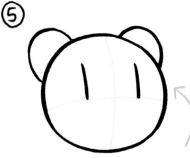

...THEN WE CAN PLACE HER EYES ALONG THE HORIZONTAL LINE!

⑥

A LITTLE TRIANGLE FOR A **NOSE**.

⑦

A BIG, SMILING **MOUTH**.

⑧

AND THEN THE COLOURED SHAPES ON HER HEAD. ONE ON HER CHEEK...

⑨

...AND ONE ON HER FOREHEAD!

NOW WE'VE DRAWN EVE'S HEAD, LET'S DRAW HER **BODY**...

10 EVE'S BODY IS A **LUMP!** LET'S DRAW HER SITTING DOWN.

11 SO WE NEED TWO CIRCLES FOR HER **FEET**, AND MAYBE SOME TUFTS OF GRASS UNDER HER BUM!

12 HER ARMS ARE **SAUSAGES** WITH LITTLE FINGERS AT THE END.

13 EVE HAS A CIRCLE ON HER BELLY, ALTHOUGH IN THIS POSE IT'S HIDDEN BY HER ARMS.

14 FINALLY, A LITTLE LUMP FOR HER **TAIL**, AND WE'VE DRAWN **METAL EVE!** EVE LIKES EXPLORING NATURE, DOING COMPLICATED MATHS, AND OCCASIONALLY TRYING TO ASSIMILATE EVERY LIVING THING.

(HOPEFULLY NOT TODAY!)

ENTER THE WORLD OF
JAMIE SMART'S

FLEMBER

DISCOVER THE MAGICAL POWER OF FLEMBER, WITH BOY-INVENTOR DEV, AND HIS BEST FRIEND BOJA THE BEAR!

JAMIE SMART'S

FLEMBER

THE SECRET BOOK

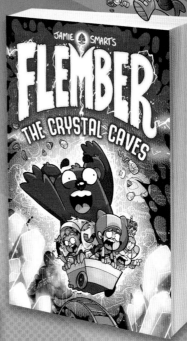

JAMIE SMART'S

FLEMBER

THE CRYSTAL CAVES

JAMIE SMART'S

FLEMBER

THE GLOWING SKULL

JAMIE SMART'S

FLEMBER

THE POWER OF THE WILDENING

ALSO
AVAILABLE

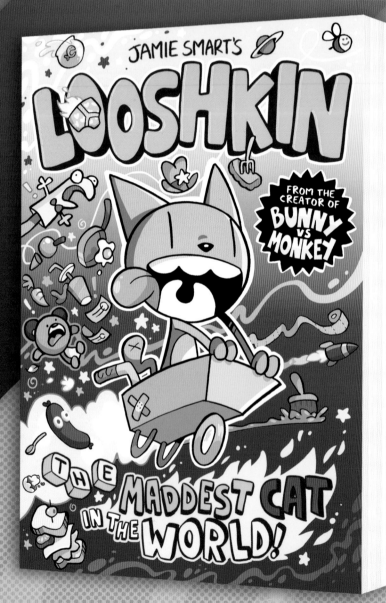

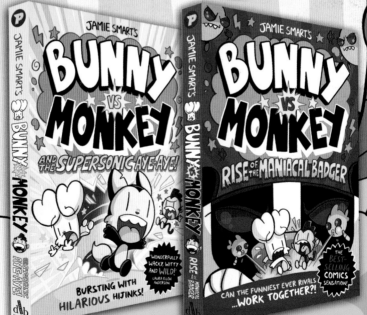

WITH EVEN MORE
COMING SOON!

SCAN THE CODE TO GO TO THEPHOENIXCOMIC.CO.UK & GET 6 ISSUES FOR £1!

JAMIE SMART HAS BEEN CREATING CHILDREN'S COMICS FOR MANY YEARS, WITH POPULAR TITLES INCLUDING *BUNNY VS MONKEY*, *LOOSHKIN* AND *FISH-HEAD STEVE*, WHICH BECAME THE FIRST WORK OF ITS KIND TO BE SHORTLISTED FOR THE ROALD DAHL FUNNY PRIZE.

THE FIRST FOUR BOOKS IN HIS *FLEMBER* SERIES OF ILLUSTRATED NOVELS ARE AVAILABLE NOW. HE ALSO WORKS ON MULTIMEDIA PROJECTS LIKE *FIND CHAFFY*.

JAMIE LIVES IN THE SOUTH-EAST OF ENGLAND, WHERE HE SPENDS HIS TIME THINKING UP STORIES AND GETTING LOST ON DOG WALKS.